Just Plain Bob

She

Let Them

A Cuckold Husband Story

Hot Wife Sharing Erotica

WARNING

This book contains sexually explicit scenes and adult language. It may be considered offensive to some readers. This book is for sale to adults ONLY.

Please store your files wisely where they cannot be accessed by underage readers.

* * * * * * * * * * * * * * * * * * *

WANT FREE COPIES OF MY BOOKS?
Just visit my blog and download free copies of my books:
awesomeauthors.org/justplainbob

About the Publisher

4Fun Publishing, a member of **BLVNP Incorporated**, 340 S. Lemon #6200, Walnut CA 91789, info@blvnp.com / legal@blvnp.com
NOTE: Due to the highly emotional reaction of some people to works of erotic fiction, any email sent to the above address that contains foul language or religious references is automatically deleted by our anti-spam software and will not be seen. All other communications are welcome.

DISCLAIMER

Please don't be stupid and kill yourself. This book is a work of FICTION. Do not try any new sexual practice that you find in this book. It is fiction and not to be confused with reality. Neither the author nor the publisher or its associates assume any responsibility for any loss, injury, death or legal consequences resulting from acting on the contents in this book. Every character in this book is over 18 years of age. The author's opinions are not to be construed as the opinions of the publisher. The material in this book is for entertainment purposes ONLY. Enjoy.

She Let Them

A Cuckold Husband Story
Hot Wife Sharing Erotica

By: Just Plain Bob

© **Just Plain Bob 2015**
ISBN: 978-1-68030-532-6

Two overheard conversations led to both the best and worst times of my life. I know it sounds confusing, but then ain't that life?

***

I wasn't even supposed to be there. I had flown to Chicago to renegotiate a contract with a supplier who had missed several delivery dates. I got to the supplier only to be told that there would be no talks because they had just filed bankruptcy. I called the airport and found that if I hustled back to the airport I could get a flight back home at eleven that morning.

I left at seven and I was back home at two. I stopped at the office to let the boss know the situation with Argus. I entered the building, took the elevator to the third floor, but decided to hit the john before reporting in to Mike.

I was sitting in the end stall when someone else came in and took the stall on the other end. I heard a cell phone ring and the guy on the other end answered it and I recognized the voice of Dan Winters.

"Hello?

"Oh hi."

"No, I don't think so. Mike sent Henry out of town again so that means he will be with Claudine tonight and tomorrow night. Hell, he might even take the day off and spend it with her."

"No way. Not without Mike."

"Okay, I'll ask him and see when he is available again, but I know that it won't be as long as Henry is gone."

"Okay. I'll check with Mike and call you back."

I heard Dan flush, go wash his hands and then leave the room. I sat there and considered what I'd just heard. My boss Mike had sent me out of town and my boss Mike was going to be spending the time I was gone with my wife Claudine. Given the tone of the conversation on Dan's side it did not seem like it would be the first time that it had happened.

And there was one other thing to consider.

There was no way that Dan could have missed the fact that my stall was occupied, but he still held a normal conversation in a normal tone of voice that meant, to me anyway, that it didn't matter if the person in my stall heard what was said. To me that said that it also didn't matter to Dan because it was common knowledge anyway. Common knowledge that could be mentioned out loud because good old Henry was not around to hear it. Henry, the poor bastard, was in Chicago. I decided that I wasn't going to check in with Mike after all. I left the building and headed for the house without bothering to call Claudine.

***

As I drove home I thought about our marriage and our relationship. I'd met Claudine in my senior year at Eastern Michigan University. It had been love at first sight on my part, but not hers. In fact it took me a dozen tries before she would agree to go out with me.

Once we started dating Claudine still dated others and I only got to go out with her two or three times a month. She told me that she wasn't going to have a relationship with any one person until she was sure she was ready to settle down and then she would narrow the field down to the ones that really interested her. I got tired of being one of many and even though I wanted her, I decided to give it up and I stopped calling her. She would take her place on that long list of things that I really wanted, but never got.

About a month before graduation I was sitting in one of the off campus coffee shops when Claudine came in, saw me and came over and asked if she could join me. I said yes and she sat down. She asked me how I'd been and I said that I was fine and then she asked why I had stopped calling her.

"I got tired of standing in line Claudine."

"That is no way to win a girl's heart Henry."

"I don't see it that way Claudine. To me I was chasing after something that did not want to be caught."

"I told you that I would eventually narrow the field Henry."

"Yes you did, but you didn't say that it would be any time soon and there was a limit to how much time I was going to spend on what might be a losing proposition."

"That isn't a very romantic attitude for a man to have."

"I didn't get a whole lot of encouragement from you Claudine. I was just one of many and you didn't treat me any different than you did any of the others so why fight it?

"You were on my short list Henry."

"But still on a list Claudine. I'm at the point in my life where I need something permanent. In just a little over three weeks I'll be out of here and I don't yet know where I'm going. I have offers from both coasts and I haven't yet made up my mind where I'm going, but I may not be around here much longer. Even if I had been on your short list at the time I gave up calling there wouldn't have been enough time left to develop the kind of relationship I want."

"Too bad Henry, it could have been." She she got up and left.

***

I too had a short list. It was of job offers I'd received after sending out resumes and going for interviews. I settled on the one in Atlanta and a week after graduation I started my new job. The first couple of weeks were spent learning my way around the job, meeting co-workers and settling into my apartment.

There were a half dozen single women where I worked and when they found out I was new to the area a couple of them offered to show me around. I took them up on the offer and dated three of them off and on. There was no spark between any of them and me and the relationships were more like good friends paling around. I did meet one woman who lived in my apartment complex and while there was no spark there either Carrie was open to a 'friends with benefits' relationship and that is what I settled for and stopped looking.

Eight months went by and then my company bought out another company. There was a lot of job duplication and a lot of the people in the purchased company were let go or offered a transfer and so it came to pass one day that I heard a familiar voice behind me say:

"Hello stranger."

I turned around and there stood Claudine smiling down at me.

To shorten the tale some Claudine and I started dating and about six months later Claudine told me she was looking for another job and when I asked why she said:

"Read the company policies and procedures manual Henry. It clearly states that family members may not work in the same department."

That was my first indication that Claudine's short list was down to just one name. She was able to work out a lateral transfer to another department and three months later we were married.

The next five years were great. We had decided to hold off on having kids until we'd had some time to go places, do some things and in general enjoy life and we did.

***

When I got home I parked one block over from the house and walked home. My plan was to sneak into the house, find a good hiding place and then catch Mike and Claudine in the act. After kicking Mike's ass I would throw Claudine out and then find myself a damned good attorney.

But catching the cheaters wasn't to be, at least not then. Claudine must have left work early because her car was already in the garage. I walked in the back door of the garage and quietly opened the connecting door from the garage to the house. I was hoping that maybe Claudine would be in the shower getting all clean and sweet smelling for her lover and that would give me an opportunity to get in the house and hide, but Claudine was in the kitchen talking on the phone. Through the cracked open door I listened in on my second one sided phone conversation of the day.

"When will you get it through your head that when I say no I mean no."

"No Mike, I don't believe you. You will lie to me and then do what you did the first time. It is bad enough that you have me cheating on Henry, but I will not do it while talking to him on the phone."

"No, damn it. No! You can come over after I've had his evening phone call and not one minute before."

"Okay. I call you as soon I've heard from him."

I quietly closed the door and went back to my car. Even though I'd heard what Dan had said there was still a small part of me that said, "No, there must be some mistake. She wouldn't do that to me." But after what I'd just heard from her own mouth there wasn't even a smidgen of denial left in my body. One thing I did know was that if Claudine wasn't going to call Mike until after she had talked to me she wouldn't be calling Mike that night.

I stopped at a gas station phone booth and looked in the Yellow Pages. It took me nine phone calls before I found a detective agency that still had someone in the office and who would agree to see me on such short notice. It cost me a premium to get them to do what I wanted, but ten minutes after Claudine left for work in the morning a man from the agency was busy wiring the house for audio and video.

An hour after he left, I called Mike on my cell phone and told him that I might have to stay in Chicago a day longer than I'd planned. I told him it looked like Argus would be closing its doors for good and that I should know in a day or so. Next I called Claudine at work and asked who she was busy talking to last night.

"I called four times and got a busy signal every time. I finally gave up and went to bed."

"I don't know why you couldn't get me honey. I wasn't on the phone at all last night. I even waited up for your call."

"No matter. I just needed to hear your voice and tell you that I love you."

"I love you too baby. Hurry home okay?"

"It looks like I'll be here until the day after tomorrow. If you have to call me do it on my cell since I might be in late, late meetings trying to solve the problems with Argus. Since I'm talking to you now I won't call again tonight. I'll call you tomorrow when I know more about when I'll be able to leave."

After that it was keep out of sight so no one could tell Claudine or Mike that I was I the area. I was parked down the street in a rental when

Claudine arrived home at five forty-five and twenty minutes later, Mike's Escalade pulled up in the driveway and he got out and went into the house. He didn't knock on the door or ring the bell, he just opened the door and walked right in. That pissed me off almost as much as the fact that he was fucking my wife. As soon as the door closed behind him, I started up and drove off.

I took in a movie that night and the next day I lounged around the motel pool for a while and then watched some TV. At one I called Mike and told him that Argus had gone belly up, but I wouldn't be able to get a flight out until the next morning. Then I called Claudine and told her the same at that it would be another day before I could get home to her. Then I told her that I wouldn't be calling her that night since I needed to get to bed early because I had to be at the airport at six a.m. for my flight.

I was parked just down the street again when Mike showed up and walked into my house. Mike didn't know it, but he was about to pay one hell of a price for stabbing me in the back. Claudine wasn't going to make out too well on the deal either.

***

Claudine left for work at seven-fifteen the next morning and at nine the man from Stillwell Investigative Services had all of his equipment out of the house. I had him leave the phone tap and when I stopped by the Stillwell offices that afternoon to pay the balance of my bill, I paid to purchase the phone tap. At two I had a DVD in my briefcase and was on my way home to view it while I waited for Claudine to come home from work.

It was an eye opener. Mike treated Claudine like shit! He pushed her around, slapped her ass, bit her nipples and when he fucked her ass he just shoved his cock in and smiled when she screamed. He grabbed a handful of her hair and jerked her head back so far that it stretched her neck as he fucked her doggie and said:

"Whose slut are you?"

"Yours baby."

"You like my cock?"

"I love your cock."

"What do you want bitch?"

"Fuck me baby, fuck me hard."

"You are mine right?"

"Oh God yes baby, I'm yours."

He was pounding into her missionary with her legs up on his shoulders when he asked:

"Who fucks you best you sleazy cunt?"

"You do baby, you know that you do."

"Better than your wimpy ass husband?"

"Much better baby. Fuck me baby, fuck me hard."

There were hours of that shit and I could look at it later. I started skipping over the fuck scenes and stopped to watch the parts where they rested up and talked.

"Have you told him that you are ready for a kid yet?"

"Just last week like you told me to."

"What did he say?"

"He said he was glad because he was ready to be a daddy."

"Well he isn't going to be one because it is going to be my kid right?"

"Yes baby, all my babies will be yours."

"You get off the pill like I told you?"

"Yes baby."

"You tell him you have gone off the pill and that he has to use a rubber. Tell him you want to plan the time of your pregnancy. When are you going to be at your most fertile again?"

"The twenty-first baby."

"So I need to get your wimp ass husband out of town say from the nineteenth until the twenty-third and then fuck you like crazy to get you pregnant. Probably should plan on taking those days as vacation days or sick leave so we can fuck up a storm and make sure that I knock you up. Sound good?"

"Yes baby. I'm already looking forward to it."

It was news to me that Claudine was ready to have a kid. She hadn't mentioned it to me. If I was ready to kill them both after hearing what they talked about on that first night, after hearing what they talked about the second night I was ready to kill them dismember them, and feed them to hungry dogs.

Mike spent the night and ripped off a piece and then told Claudine to plan on having a 'motel lunch' with him that afternoon.

"I want your mouth coated with my cum when you kiss him when he gets home. I want your cunt full of my cum and before you fuck him I want you to make him eat your pussy so he can taste me."

"Yes baby."

"Call me when he falls asleep and tell me what his face looked like when he lapped me up. If he wants to know why you are so wet tell him it is because you have gotten so horny waiting for him to get back. You got that?"

"Whatever you want baby."

"God, but you are such a slut."

"I'm a slut baby, but I'm your slut."

"Yes you are and don't you forget it bitch."

***

I had the DVD hidden away and dinner on the stove when Claudine got home. I wasn't ready to confront her yet so when she ran up to me and threw her arms around me and went to kiss me I steeled myself for it and hoped that I wouldn't barf, but I was surprised. I knew what cum tasted like – mine anyway – since I had kissed Claudine after she had given me head, but when she kissed me what I tasted was Crest toothpaste. It seemed that regardless of Mike had told her to do she had stopped on the way home and brushed her teeth. When she broke the kiss she said:

"Can dinner wait? I'm horny as hell."

"I guess it can wait."

"Good. Turn it down low or turn it off so it doesn't burn while I run up and take a quick shower. Meet you on the bed in five okay?"

"You got it."

So much for me soaking my cock in Mike's dick snot. The only reason for Claudine to take a shower just home from work would be to clean Mike's gunk out of her.

She was naked on the bed when I got there and as soon as I stripped, I got on the bed and moved to go down on her just to see what she would do. As I moved into position she said:

"Not tonight honey, I'm horny and I need you in me. Hurry honey, make love to me. I need it bad."

After we had finished she wouldn't let me go sixty-nine with her either. "No honey, not tonight. I want to concentrate on you."

I wondered what was going on. She didn't do any of the things that Mike had told her to do and that she had told him she would do. She got me up and we went a second time and then went down to dinner. She brought me up to date on all the latest gossip that I had missed by being gone and then we did the dishes, watched some TV and then went up to bed. She got me hard and we went one more time then she snuggled in next to me and we fell asleep. I slept soundly and I didn't know if she got up and called Mike or not. The telephone tap would answer that question for me.

The next day was Saturday and it was the once a month when Claudine went and had her hair done. As soon as she was gone I checked the medicine cabinet in the bathroom. After I had watched the DVD, I'd gone into the bathroom and checked out Claudine's birth control pill holder. I had counted them and the count was down one from the previous day so she was lying to Mike about going off the pill. Next I pulled the tape out of the recorder on the phone line and listened to it.

"He's sound asleep."

"Did you do what I told you?"

"Of course I did."

"What happened?"

"When I kissed him he made a face and asked me what I'd had for lunch. I couldn't tell him it was your cock so I told him it was fish and he told me that I should go brush my teeth."

"How did you end up with a clueless clown like him?"

"He's not all that bad."

"He just can't take care of you like I can is that it? Did you have him eat your snatch?"

"He was reluctant, but I said 'no eatee, no fuckee' and he made a hell of a face when he did it, but he didn't say anything."

"Of course not. He's clueless."

"Good thing for us baby. If he wasn't clueless we could end up being caught. He did piss and moan when I made him wear the condoms I bought on the way home. I almost thought he wouldn't make love to me. I did get him to buy the story that I didn't want to take chances until I could plan the time. I told him no way I wanted to find myself eight months pregnant in the winter and he seemed to accept that."

"Have you figured out yet how you are going to get him to go along with naming it Michael if it is a boy and Michelle if it is a girl?"

"No, but we have plenty of time before we get to that point."

"I want you to find a way to spend an hour or two with me on Tuesday."

"I'll try."

"Try my ass you slut! You will do it."

"Yes baby. I guess I'll just have to tell him I have to work late. It is a good thing he never checks on that."

"I keep telling you, the man is clueless."

There was more, but that was the meat of it. I wondered how it had started and how long it had been going on. Not that it mattered. It had started and it was going on and as a result there was going to be a whole lot of hurting going on because of it.

***

Monday I made an appointment with an attorney and I was in his office Tuesday afternoon when I got the call from Claudine telling me that she was going to be working late. I'd already played the tape for the attorney so we both knew what 'late' meant.

The mechanics were cut and dry. It was a no-fault state so the assets were going to be split fifty/fifty and we both made comparable wages so there would be no alimony. Where I would make out on the deal was that our state was one that allowed alienation of affection suits and – and this was the biggie – Mike was over my department and Claudine's department and our company policy and procedures manual was quite specific when it came to relationships between supervisors and subordinates. Mike having anything at all to do with Claudine was a very big no-no and his sending me out of town so they could be together was the kiss of death so in addition to suing Mike for alienation of affections I would be suing to company for failing to enforce the CP&P.

At the very least Mike and Claudine would be joining the ranks of the unemployed and the chances were better than good that the company would settle the suit to keep things from going public. I wouldn't be able to work there any more after I sued, but given that I figured that everyone I worked with – evidenced by Dan's phone call – knew that I was being fucked over and kept quiet about it I didn't want to stay there and work with the assholes anyway.

It was all worked out before I left the attorney's office. Mike, Claudine and the company would all be served Friday morning. The company, in the person of Marge Bishop, the manager of Human Resources, would be served first and then Mike and then Claudine. It was set up that way in the hopes that Marge would get right on the phone to Mike and would be talking to him when the process server walked up to his desk. Mike would know who the guy was and what was going to happen to him as soon as he hung up the phone. The timing was set for eleven am since I had a standing lunch date with Claudine every Friday at noon. That way I could save a few bucks not having to buy the cunt a meal.

When I walked out of the office, I saw a woman sitting in the reception area. Our eyes met and she gave me a nervous smile and looked away from me. She looked familiar to me. I'd seen her some place, but it wouldn't come to me. Oh well, stuff like that happens and I knew it would sit in the back of my mind and bug me until I could place her.

My kiss from Claudine that night tasted of Crest again and again she wouldn't let me go down on her because she claimed she had a yeast infection but she offered to take care of me with her mouth. I let her bring me off that way – twice – and then we fell asleep. She did get up and call Mike after I fell asleep. I checked the recorder the next day and it was pretty much a repeat of the last call I listened to. She told him about doing all of all the things she did that he told her to do that she didn't do. Yes, she had frenched me with her cum coated mouth and yes, she had me eat her pussy and suck all of his gunk out of her before fucking me and then had to fake an orgasm because I just couldn't get her off like he could.

They talked about what they would be doing on my next trip and talked about Claudine sneaking away for a quickie on Saturday or Sunday. They didn't know it, but there would be no reason for them to sneak around after Friday.

Wednesday when Claudine got home she told me she had gone to the drug store over lunch and got a self-test kit and she found out she didn't have a yeast infection after all and did that give me any ideas?" It did and I took advantage of the fact that I had only two more nights and then she would be history and I would have to start looking for her replacement.

I had no idea what was going on with Claudine. No change in the quantity or quality of our love making and no signs that she was unhappy with me. The love and affection all seemed to be there so what was she doing with Mike? And what was with all the lying to him about what she was doing to me at his direction? Well, he wasn't married so she could move in with him after her rude awakening on Friday.

***

At nine Friday morning I told Mike that I had a doctor's appointment at ten and depending on the outcome I might not be back. I wished I could have been someplace where I could have seen him when he was served. The guy serving the papers worked for the attorney and he had been instructed to hand the papers to Mike and say:

"Clueless said for me to tell you to have a nice day."

But I needed to get home and have all of Claudine's stuff packed and ready when she rushed home after being served. I left at ten and went home and started packing Claudine's stuff and moving it out into the garage. I was about a third of the way done when my cell went off. I looked at my watch and saw that it was ten after eleven and that the call was from Claudine. I smiled and let the call and the next dozen go to voice mail. Then the home phone rang and I answered it.

"Hello?"

"Henry? What are you doing home and what is the meaning of these divorce papers? And what the hell is this garbage about adultery?"

"Well first of all what you have been doing with Mike is adultery and what you were doing with Mike is why I am divorcing you. As for what I am doing here at home, I am packing your stuff and moving it out into the garage where it will be when you come to pick it up."

"Just wait Henry. Don't do anything until I get there. We need to talk honey. It isn't what you think it is. I'm leaving right now and I'm heading straight home. I love you Henry. Don't doubt that. Don't ever doubt that."

She hung up before I could tell her not to bother because it would be a waste of time. I went into the den and got a copy of the DVD, put it in the player, turned on the TV and then went back to work packing up Claudine's belongings.

I heard her when she came into the house and went downstairs. She rushed up to me and tried to put her arms around me, but I pushed her away. I took her arm and led her over to the couch, pushed her down on it and then walked over to the player and pushed the 'play' button.

"You sit here and watch this until it is over and then I'll listen to what you have to say, but I'll tell you ahead of time that you will be pretty much wasting your breath."

Five minutes later she walked into the bedroom, but before she could say a word I said:

"I said watch it until it was over and then I'd listen. You still have another forty minutes to go. Be thankful I'm only making you watch the highlights instead of the hours and hours I had to watch."

"I don't need to watch it. I was there. I know what took place."

"Then why are you here wasting my time?"

"Because it isn't what you think and I have to let you know that."

"What am I, stupid? I have hours and hours of you fucking that dirt bag and it isn't what I think? It was all done with special effects? That wasn't his cock going into your body? That wasn't you, just your head photo shopped or magically transposed onto someone else's body?"

"Don't be sarcastic Henry. What I mean is that it had nothing to do with you or us. I love you Henry and I always have. Mike shouldn't have happened, but he did and I ended up liking what I got from him so I kept seeing him. I don't love him Henry and in fact most of the time I don't even like him all that much. He was never a threat to you Henry. I'm yours and I always will be yours."

I laughed at that and then said, "How can something that shouldn't have happened happen and then continue happening?"

"I dated Mike maybe a half dozen times after I first got here and before you and I got together. We did make out several times and one or two of them got pretty hot and heavy, but I wouldn't put out for him and he has always called me a cock teaser. At the last company Christmas party I had a bunch to drink – you remember, you laughed at the way I as acting – and I was feeling good and having a great time. I' danced with everyone in the department and when it was Mike's turn, he maneuvered me under the mistletoe and kissed me. It shouldn't have been a biggie, almost every guy there did the same thing. But Mike slipped me some tongue when he kissed me. I was in a mellow mood so I gave him a little back and then he walked me back to our table.

"Maybe half an hour later, I got up to use the bathroom and when I came out and was heading back to our table, a door opened, a hand grabbed my arm, and pulled me into a dark room. I was spun around and bent over a desk and then my skirt was up around my waist, my panties pushed to one side and a cock was pushed into me. I thought it was you. I thought you were being a little bit kinky and I started pushing back and asking you to fuck me and fuck me hard. I got pounded harder and harder and I really got into it. I was pushing back and moaning, "Fuck me, fuck me harder, make me cum, make me cum." I started to orgasm when I heard:

"I always knew you were a slut."

"It wasn't your voice. That's the first that I knew it wasn't you. He pulled out of me, spun me around and pushed me to my knees in front of him and told me to clean him off with my mouth. I told him to fuck off and die and start running because you were going to hurt him bad when I told you that he had raped me. He laughed and asked just who you would be maddest at and he played back all of my "Fuck me, fuck me harder's." He had recorded it on his cell phone. I didn't believe that you could hear them and believe that it was a rape. Then he told me to get busy and clean him up. I wasn't happy about, but I didn't believe that I had a choice so I did it.

"After that night I steered clear of him, but five weeks later when you were out of town a bunch of us stopped at Toby's for drinks after work. Mike came in and about an hour later he came up to me, leaned down and whispered, "Let's go." I told him that I wasn't going to go anywhere with him and he smiled and said:

"Okay slut, let's see what your co-workers have to say after they hear this."

He brought out his cell phone, but before he could push the button to play it I said, "Don't." I grabbed my purse and followed him out to the parking lot. He told me to get on the back seat of his car and I told him no. He said:

"Do it slut, or when your hubby gets home I'll play this on the loudspeaker system at work and everybody including your husband will hear you begging me to fuck you."

"I got on the back seat and he pulled out his cock and told me to suck it. As I bent to take him in my mouth several of the people from work left the bar to go home and they walked by Mike's car and saw what was going on. Mike saw them and laughed.

"Still think hubby will buy the rape story? With all the witnesses that saw you leave the bar with me willingly?"

"He had me suck him off in the car and then he drove me home and fucked me off and on all night long. In the morning he made a point of playing his cell phone for me. The bastard had set the damned thing to record and had put it on the bedside stand and had recorded what we did. You know me Henry and how I am when it comes to sex. Once I gave in and he got me going I hollered, screamed and moaned just like I do when you get me going. He drove me to the bar to pick up my car and told me that he was going to spend the night with me every night you were gone and if I gave him any shit over it he would play the damned recording on his cell for anybody who wanted to listen. After that whenever he crooked his finger I went.

"There was something of the submissive in me that I never knew was there and he found it. Mike treated me like a dog and I liked it. He bossed me around, physically abused me and I liked it. His love making was rough and I ate it up, but I swear to you Henry that he was no threat to you. He would tell me to do things to you and I always told him that I would, but I never did. I loved you too much to do any of those things to you. I have a travel kit in my car and I always stopped at a gas station and douched and cleaned myself before coming home to you. I never had any of him in me when I made love to you Henry. I gargled and brushed my teeth before I would kiss you.

"I fucked him because I was always afraid of what he would do if I said no and yes, I liked it, but I would have stopped in a heartbeat if I could have gotten my hands on that damned cell phone and destroyed it. I love you Henry, honest to God I do."

"But not enough to trust me. You should have come to me at that Christmas party. You should have trusted me and my love for you, but you didn't. Because you didn't, all of the people I work with are laughing at the clueless cuckold behind his back. I'm a fucking joke at work and every one there knows that Mike is between your legs as soon as he can get me out of town. But then I wasn't out of town Tuesday was I? You have humiliated me in front of everybody Claudine and it doesn't matter why you did it. The only thing that matters is that you did do it and you continued doing it and you would have continued doing it if I had not found out. I have no room in my life for an unfaithful wife. So, if you have finished with what you came here to say you can start taking some of your stuff out to your car."

"Why should I leave? This house is as much mine as it is yours."

"Because I have no place to go, but you do. You can go live with your lover. Of course the real reason is that given the way I feel about things right now there is a very good chance that I will hurt you if you try and stay here."

"Who do you think you are kidding Henry? You are not the type to hurt me or any other woman."

"The old Henry never would have, but you and Mike created a new Henry and even I don't know how the new Henry is going to behave. He has a lot of rage built up inside of him and it needs to be released. Being around when it happens would probably not be a good thing. Just go Claudine. I don't want to look at you. I don't want to hear your voice. I don't want to smell you. Just fucking leave."

She looked at me, tears starting to run down her cheeks. She started to say something and I screamed at her, "GET THE FUCK OUT OF HERE!"

She ran from the room and I went back to stuffing her shit into plastic bags.

***

I spent the weekend doing odd jobs around the house. Fixing things to make it look better when I put it up for sale. Claudine might want to buy me out and keep the place, but I sure didn't want it after seeing Mike in my bedroom. But even if Claudine wanted it I would still need to get a market appraisal so I stayed busy cleaning and fixing the place up so it would look good for the realtor.

I had no idea what I would be facing when I went to work on Monday. What I got wasn't anywhere near what I expected. When I stepped off the elevator and headed for my desk Dan Winters stood up and started to clap and then everyone in the room was standing and clapping. Dan walked up to me and said:

"Let me buy you a cup of coffee."

He led me to the break room, we got coffee and sat down at a table and Sherri Gossett walked up and joined us. Sherri looked at Dan and he nodded and Sherri said:

"We have been elected to apologize for the group."

"Apologize? What for?"

"For keeping quiet about what was going on between Mike and Claudine. We didn't know what the situation was so we kept quiet."

"The situation? I don't understand."

"We didn't know if you knew or not and we didn't want to interfere."

I guess they saw the confusion on my face because Dan said, "We didn't think you were really that kind of guy, but there are guys who get off on their women playing with other men and guys who like to watch their wives with other men and there are what are called open marriages and there are people who are swingers. We didn't know if that was what was going on or not so we just kept quiet. It wasn't until we noticed that it only happened when you were out of town that we began to suspect that you had no idea what was going on."

I looked from Dan to Sherri and I guess they still saw that I was still trying to figure out what they were trying to say so Sherri said:

"We decided that we had to let you know, but in such a way that if you didn't know we could let you know and if you did know we wouldn't embarrass you by asking you about it face to face."

Dan took over and said. "I knew you were supposed to be in Chicago when I saw you go into the bathroom so I followed you in and faked the phone call that you overheard. If you knew there was no face to face that could cause embarrassment and if you didn't it would have clued you in. We got our answer on Friday when Mike and Claudine were served. The icing on the cake was the company getting served also. Mike was called into the office and suspended without pay pending investigation of the allegations you made. That's what the greeting you got this morning was all about, getting rid of the asshole as well as suing him."

Sherri said, "They sent him home at one and by three everyone in the office had been called in and asked if they knew what was going on. Management is severally pissed at most of us right now. They say that by not letting them know we opened them up to your law suit. I expect that when the big cheeses get here this morning you will be called in."

"I planned on seeing Markman first thing and giving him my letter of resignation. As far as talking to him is concerned I've already been told by my attorney to refer any questions to him."

"Why are you resigning?"

"After overhearing that phone call I figured that everyone here knew what was going on and were laughing at me behind my back and no way could I keep working with a bunch assholes like that."

"We don't want you to resign."

"Might not have any choice in the matter. Not likely that they will keep me around since I'm suing them. Another reason for the resignation is so I can leave on my own terms rather than be terminated on some trumped up bullshit that would be used to cover up the real reason for my being fired."

I looked at my watch and said that I'd better be getting to my desk. I stood up and offered my hand to Dan. "Thanks for the heads up." We shook hands and I gave Sherri a hug and went to my desk.

At nine-fifteen, I was called into Markman's office and I handed him my letter of resignation. He asked me what it was and he asked why and I told him. He gave it back to me and told me that they would never do something like that.

"Besides, we have plans for you. We want you to take Mike's position. He is gone you know. We will want to discuss your lawsuit, but I understand that we will need to set up something with your attorney so we can do that."

The rest was anti-climatic. Mike and Claudine were fired. The attorney and the company worked it out that the company would pick up my attorney's tab and I would drop the lawsuit. I got Mike's job which came with an eighteen thousand dollar a year raise. Claudine didn't fight the divorce and she didn't want the house so it was sold. I haven't seen or heard from her since the day I handed her the check for her share of the sale of the house. Mike settled the alienation lawsuit (he had to sell his house to come up with the money) and with that money and my share of the sale of the house I bought an upscale condo at Wintergreen Estates.

One day Mike answered a knock on his apartment door and received a fist in his face from a man in a ski mask. He fell to the floor and his unknown assailant did a number on his private parts with a pair of steel toed boots. A neighbor coming home from a night out on the town found him curled up in a ball and called 911. For some strange reason a pair of detectives came to visit me and asked me if I could shed any light on the matter, but all I could do was echo Sgt. Schultz's immortal words.

"I know nothing."

When they asked me if I could account for my time the night it happened to poor Mike I told them that I had just been keeping company with my TV set.

"So you have no alibi for the time?"

"Alibi? Why the hell should I need an alibi?"

I understand the case is still open.

Anyway, that was the story on the worst part. The best part started around the time of the start of the divorce.

***

It was about three months from my divorce being final and although I'd sold the house I was still living in it waiting on the closing date. I was driving to work and I saw a woman struggling to change a flat tire and I pulled over to see if I could be of any help. She looked familiar and it wasn't until I was letting the car down off the jack that I remembered who she was. She was the woman who had given me the nervous smile when I was last at my attorney's office.

As I was putting the jack and the flat into the truck she thanked me for my help and offered to pay me for my help. I told her she could buy me a cup of coffee and a sweet roll at the Denny's that was just across the street and she smiled and told me that I had a deal. We introduced ourselves as we walked across the street to the restaurant. Her name was Tammi. As we sat down she said:

"I have the feeling that I know you from somewhere."

"I chuckled and said, "That's the feeling I had when I saw you in my attorney's office."

"That's right! That is where I saw you."

"But when I saw you there I had the feeling that I had seen you somewhere before. Do you live in this area?"

"The twelve hundred block of Wilcox."

"That's just six blocks from me. I probably saw you out walking or in one of the local stores. If I'm not hitting on a sore subject what did you need legal help with?"

"Getting rid of an abusive husband. You?"

"Getting rid of a wayward wife."

"Making any progress?"

"Should be final in another sixty days."

"That quick?"

"She isn't fighting it."

"Wish I could say the same."

"Not going smooth I take it?"

"Jules isn't fighting the divorce itself, but he has spent months fighting over every stick of furniture, every nickel and dime and who gets what photos out of the photo albums. He is even fighting over who gets the fish in the aquarium."

"Not meaning to get too personal here, but why don't you just say to hell with it and let him have what he wants? For one thing, if you keep it around after him making such a fuss over it, it will only remind you of him. The other thing is that he is probably just fighting over the stuff to piss you off. Take that away from him. Or you could give him part of what he wants."

"What do you mean by that?"

"You are fighting over the coffee table? Cut it in half with a chain saw and give him his half. Photos in the album? Cut everything you don't want him to have out of the pictures and then give him the albums. I don't know much about aquariums, but I can't see where you could come up with any great degree of affection for the fish in it. Unplug it and let it sit for a couple of days and then tell him to come and get it or better yet have it delivered to him."

"I don't know that I can be that mean and nasty."

"It isn't mean or nasty. All you would be doing is giving him back what he is giving you. All he is doing is deliberately trying to piss you off. He is having fun making you suffer. Do you honestly think he gives a rat's ass about an easy chair or a fish? Why waste your energy playing his game? You can buy a new coffee table and one without his memory attached to it. You can copy the photo albums before you give them to him and you can replace the goldfish for a buck apiece. The object of the divorce is to get rid of him. Letting him stay around and continuously fight over stuff that doesn't mean squat in the long run, it just doesn't make any sense."

"You would think that my lawyer should have told me that."

"Why would he? He became a lawyer because as a lawyer he could make good money. He might be working for you to get you your divorce, but the longer it drags out the higher his bill. Why would he care if you and hubby want to fight over furniture and drag out the process?"

"I guess I should have had a flat tire sooner."

"I have lots more good ideas if you would like to talk about them over dinner tonight."

It was a shot in the dark and I had no expectation of success, but she surprised me and said that she would like that very much. When I picked her up at seven I was again surprised. When she had said the twelve hundred block of Wilcox it hadn't registered on me, but that was a pretty exclusive neighborhood. The house I walked up to had to be in the million five range and I wondered why she hadn't mentioned the house in the squabbles she was having with her ex.

We ate at Alfredo's and over veal scaloppini and Chianti I told her my story and got hers. Hers was simple. Her husband got violent when he drank and more often than not she ended up his punching bag. He was always guilt ridden and apologetic the next day and swore that it would never happen again if she would forgive him, but of course it did until she had finally had enough.

She had called the cops several times on him so his abuse was on record when the final time came. He beat on her and passed out, she called the cops and he woke up in jail. She refused to bail him out and when he was released he was served with divorce papers and a restraining order which he promptly violated. He came to the house drunk, hit her several times and then passed out again. She took a cast iron frying pan and beat the fuck out of him with it and he woke up in the hospital. When he was released he was given ninety days for contempt of court for violating the restraining order. He was warned when he was released that the next time it would be six months and a third time would get him a year. He decided that he didn't like jail and settled for harassing her over furniture.

After dinner, I suggested going next door to the Black Mushroom for drinks and a dance or two and she said okay. I got her home about one in the morning and walked her to her door. I told her that I had enjoyed myself and that I would like to do it again and then she asked:

"Can you do me a favor and kiss me?"

"I'd love to, but why is that doing you a favor?"

"Don't look, but just down the street is a red and white Ford F-150. I want the asshole to see you with my tongue halfway down your throat."

"Shouldn't you be inside calling the cops?"

"I can't. The restraining order says five hundred feet and where he is sitting is five hundred and twenty-five feet. I know because I've measured it."

"What if he gets pissed and says to hell with the restraining order?"

She opened her purse and showed me the Llama .380 she had in it and said:

"I'd almost welcome it if he did."

I took her in my arms and kissed her. It was a long one and she held nothing back. When we broke the kiss she said, "Call me." And she went inside.

I made it a point to avoid looking at the pick-up truck when I pulled out and left. I wasn't at all surprised when the truck pulled away from the curb and followed me to my place. He didn't slow down as he drove by but I would bet that he memorized my address. It would be interesting to see what he would do with it.

I dated Tammi three times over the next two weeks and I learned a little more about her. She owned her home outright and it was hers before she married Jules so he had no claim on it. She was what she called a 'trust fund baby' in that her parents and grandparents had been very wealthy and they had set up several trust funds for her that she came into when she turned twenty-one. I also found out that she worked as an unpaid volunteer for several of the charities in town.

Each date ended with one of her hot kisses and on two of the three dates the F-150 followed me home. I was on the edge of sticking my nose into Tammi's business and calling the police on her ex for stalking along with giving them notice that if they didn't do something about it I would when suddenly it didn't matter anymore.

I had a date with Tammi on Wednesday and we did the kiss thing for the asshole in the F-150 and then I left, but this time he didn't follow me. I didn't think anything of it figuring that by then he knew who I was and where I lived. I got a phone call from Tammi at work at nine-thirty. She wanted to know if I could come down to the police station and pick her up and give her a ride home. I asked what was up and she told me that she would tell me when I got there.

It turned out that there would be no more arguments over furniture or fish. Ten minutes after I had left her place her about to be ex kicked in her front door and three steps into the house Tammi had put six .380 holes in his chest. The EMTs who hauled him away said he smelled like the inside of a whiskey barrel. She had called her attorney while waiting for the police to respond to her call and she had spent most of the night at the station going over her story with the detectives. When it was over she was asked not to leave town and told that she might still have to talk to someone from the district attorney's office. Her attorney told her that she had nothing to worry about and had offered to give her a lift home, but she decided that she would rather call me.

As we pulled away from the station house, she asked me to take her to a motel.

"I can't face the house right now. There is blood that needs to be cleaned up and right now I just can't deal with it."

"No motel. I'll take you to my place. I don't think you need to be alone for a bit."

She didn't protest so I took her to my place, fed her some breakfast, and showed her to the master bedroom. I got her a nightgown that I had overlooked when I had packed Claudine's stuff, showed her where things were and then told her:

"Get some rest and if you need anything just give a shout."

She turned to me and said, "I do need something. I need to be held."

I kicked off my shoes and lay down on the bed with her and held her until she fell asleep. I eased my way away from her, went to the phone and called my secretary and told her that I wouldn't be back that day and then I stripped down to my boxers and got back in bed and cuddled up to Tammi.

I woke up to a very pleasant sensation and I found that Tammi had my cock out of my boxers and was holding it in one hand while licking it. I moved and she looked up at me.

"We would have reached this point sooner or later, but I need it now."

She had already taken off the nightgown and she moved over me. She took me in her right hand, lined me up, but then stopped and said:

"Last chance to say no."

I grabbed her hips and pulled her down on me and then I took my hands off of her and let her go. She rode herself to two orgasms and then I put my arms around her, rolled her onto her back and gave her a third orgasm on the way to getting mine.

When it was over she said, "I'm sorry. You must think I'm a slut, but it has been six months for me and when I woke up you had morning wood or maybe I should call it afternoon wood and I just couldn't help myself."

I kissed her forehead and said, "I don't think you are a slut. I needed it just as bad as you did, but I had intended to wait until my divorce was final. I'm a little old fashioned about some things and I did make some vows when I married and I'd thought I should keep them until I was legally released from them."

"Oh God Henry, I'm so sorry. I didn't know."

"No harm done sweetie. You did say that we would get to this point sooner or later and while I wasn't all that sure that it would happen I certainly wanted it to."

We showered together and that led us back to bed which meant another shower only that time I told her to go by herself or we would never get out of the bedroom. She smiled at me and said:

"That's a bad thing?"

While she showered, I fixed us something to eat. We ate and then I showered. After dressing I got the Yellow Pages and went looking. Believe it or not there are companies that clean up crime scenes and I found one that could have a crew at Tammi's the next morning. We set a time to meet them and then I asked Tammi how she wanted to kill time until the next day. She told me that she needed to call her attorney and let him know of her new circumstances. She called him and he told her to come down to his office and sign some papers. I drove her over to her place and dropped her off to get her car and told her that I would have dinner ready at seven. She kissed me and then said:

"I have a favor to ask."

"Ask it."

"I don't want to go into the house, but I need a change of clothes and some other things. Would you please go in there and get them for me?"

I told her that I would and she gave me a list, told me where to find them, kissed me again, and drove off to her appointment. When I got to the front door, I saw that the door jamb was splintered where he had kicked the door open and I also saw that the screen door had three holes in it. The Llama .380 had a seven shot clip and if Tammi had put six into her ex's chest a couple of them must have gone through him. I never thought that a cartridge that small could have that much power.

I wasn't sure about the legalities of stepping over the crime scene tape, but Tammi did need some of her things so I opened the door and went inside and immediately saw the large red stain on the floor. I worked my way around it, found the suitcases where Tammi said they would be. I found the items that she wanted and then I got out. When she got to my place I told her to call the detective in charge of her case and find out about the crime scene tape so we could let the clean-up crew know if they could get in the house the next morning or should we reschedule. She did and was told that the tape would be removed by morning.

After dinner we sat in front of the fireplace, sipped wine, and talked until bedtime. I offered her the spare bedroom and she told me that she would rather have a warm body near. We undressed and she looked at me with a questioning look on her face and I knew what it meant.

"I'm taking my cues from you Tammi. You get to set the scene."

She smiled and said, "In that case there really isn't any doubt, is there?"

It was a very exhausting night.

In the morning I told her to sleep in and I went over to her place and let the cleaning crew in. I was looking at the door jamb trying to figure out what I would need to fix it when the clean-up crew supervisor came up to me and told me that fixing the door and replacing the screen in the screen door were part of what they did. I gave him my cell number and told him to give me a call when they were done and he told me that they would be out of there by six that evening, but that it would be best to give the carpet at least twenty-four hours before walking on it.

**

The next day, Tammi's home was ready for her to go back to, but even so she spent two out of every three nights with me at my place until I told her the closing was upon me and that I was going to have to start looking for an apartment.

"Nonsense. I have plenty of room and we are spending most of our time together anyway so it just makes sense for you to move in with me."

She had a point and so I moved in with her. I dreaded going to the closing on the house. Claudine would be there since the house was in both of our names and her signature would be needed on the papers. She had called me at least once a week since she'd moved out, asking me to reconsider and to cancel the divorce. I kept saying no and she kept telling me that she loved me and that we could make it if only I would give her a chance. It was hard on me because I know that she did love me and I did miss her at times, but there just wasn't any way that we could be together and make it work. The night of the Christmas party we probably could have worked through, but not the rest of it. Love her, miss her and yes, even want her, but there was no way I could ever forgive or forget what she had done.

She was there and I could see that she had taken the time to make sure that she would be heart-stoppingly beautiful for the meeting. She was waiting for me outside the room where the closing would take place. She smiled at me and said:

"We could leave and skip the closing Henry. I could be moved back in by tomorrow."

I could have smiled, shrugged and walked by her and into the room without a word, but I did feel the need to hurt the woman who had ripped out my heart and so I said:

"Sure Claudine, and then I could spend all my time trying to catch you with whoever you found to take Mike's place. Doesn't sound much like the kind of life I want to lead so thanks, but no thanks. I think I'll pass on your idea." I walked by her and into the room.

The signing went off okay and we each left with a check for forty-three thousand dollars. She had been fired along with Mike and she had sued the company claiming sexual harassment. She claimed that Mike blackmailed her by telling her that if she didn't give in to him he would fire me and that the company knew what Mike was doing with her and did nothing to stop it. The company settled with her for an undisclosed sum. She left town the day after the closing and hasn't been heard from since.

***

The day my divorce was final Tammi and I went out to celebrate. We had dinner and then stopped at The Cave for some drinks and dancing. When we got home she fucked me into exhaustion and we fell asleep wrapped around each other. In the morning Tammi asked me what I planned to do now that I was single again.

"I'll enjoy the few days of freedom that I have until I can change my status back to married."

"A few days of freedom?"

"Well let's see. We have to have the blood test results before we can get the license and then there is a three day waiting period after we get the license so I'm guessing that I will be a free man for maybe eight to ten days. Oh wait! I forgot part of it. Will you marry me? I will of course sign a pre-nup."

Her face lost its smile and she said, "We have a wonderful relationship and I'm really very happy with things the way they are."

"I take it that's a no?"

"A no to marriage Henry, not a no to what we have going for us now."

"I don't understand Tammi, if what we have is fine what is wrong with making it legal?"

"Marriage changes things Henry and not always for the good."

"Is this about Jules?"

"He was everything a girl could want Henry. The nine months we were together before getting married were perfect. The first two years after we were married were marvelous and then Jules changed and the last three were an absolute hell. What we have is working Henry so let's leave it be."

She had said no so I dropped it, but just as she was afraid that marriage would change things her "no" also changed things. I liked to think that I was a pretty level headed guy and while a part of my mind understood what Tammi was saying, I am human with all of the inherent flaws that humans have. The part of my mind that understood where Tammi was coming from was a very small part of my mind. Much larger parts saw thing differently. One part saw her no as rejection of me personally. Another part saw me lumped together with Jules and Jules had become an asshole after she married him so I would become an asshole too. Another piece saw her rejection of me as her keeping my gold digging hands off of the money in her trust fund and still another saw the rejection as Tammi seeing flaws in me that she did not like.

***

Slowly our relationship began to change and from where I stood I could only see it going downhill. I decided that before I let things get to the point where we wouldn't even be friends I'd make a change.

Friday over dinner, I told Tammi that I was going to start looking for an apartment the next day.

"There is no need for that Henry. Things are fine."

"No they aren't Tammi. Maybe you haven't seen it yet, but I have."

I told her exactly what I had been thinking and that the time for me to get out would be while we were still friends.

"I don't want you to leave Henry. I know you will never be like Jules and I know you aren't after me for my money. I just don't want to get married. We can live happily together for the rest of our lives Henry and marriage won't make it any better than it is right now."

"Maybe not Tammi, but in the back of my mind is the thought that you won't marry me because there is something wrong with me, something that you don't like and can't or won't bring yourself to mention. It will lie there and fester and eat at me and cause God only knows what and like I just said, I would rather end things while we can still stay friends."

She stared at me for almost a minute and then said, "You are forcing me to do something that I had hoped that I would never have to do. Show you the reason why I can't marry you. Go out to the family room and sit down on the couch and I'll be there in a minute."

"What? Why? I mean why should you need to show me anything?"

"Just go and sit down. It will all be clear in just a minute."

I went out and sat down on the couch and a couple of minutes later Tammi came into the room with a travel case.

"I never told you what turned Jules into an abusive drunk. While I said that I knew that you would never be like Jules I meant it from the standpoint of believing that you would never become an abuser, but I do believe that you would become just as disgusted with me as Jules did."

She reached into the travel case and brought out a half dozen VHS video cassettes, turned on the TV and pushed one of the tapes into the player.

"Before I show you this I have to tell you a little story. Once upon a time a poor little rich girl rebelled against her overly controlling and restrictive parents. She was tired of being sent off to the "right" schools and of only being allowed to associate with the "right" people. "Right" being defined by her parents of course. She was only allowed to dress with the proper clothing – again, proper being defined by her parents - and anything that she decided that she liked and purchased for herself that her parents didn't like was confiscated and disposed of.

"This went on for years and might have gone on for several more had not her parents introduced her to her husband to be. They had decided that he was "right" for her and they just naturally assumed that she would accept it as she had everything else. Her mother actually started planning the wedding on the night that the poor little rich girl was introduced to her intended – a man she had never seen before in her life. It was too much for her. The next day she cleaned out her mother's jewelry box and loaded several pawnable items into her car, drove into town, hit half a dozen pawn shops and then took the money and headed west. She did mail the pawn tickets home so the purloined goods could be redeemed.

"She ended up in Los Angeles, fell in with the wrong crowd, started doing drugs, and became the poster girl for "Wild Child." She did a lot of things that were a real kick at the time. A lot of it for no other reason than to spite her parents. She eventually came to her senses, came home and healed the breach with her family. She met a wonderful man, married him and life was perfect until she came home one day and found her husband sitting on the couch right where you are now and watching this."

She pushed the play button. A title flashed on the screen, "The Wayward Teen" and it was followed by the credits listing several well known male porn stars and "introducing Sunny Daze." The opening scene was of a young girl standing by the side of the road in a school girl's uniform with her thumb out hitch hiking. A car stopped, driven by Hershel Savage, and the girl was offered a ride. A comment was made by Savage that "It's only fair that since I'm giving you a ride you should give me one too." The next scene was Savage driving his cock into the girl who was still wearing her catholic school girl's uniform. T.T.Boy walked in on the two and joined in. The girl had Savage in her mouth and Boy in her pussy when Tom Byron walked in. Then it was Savage in her pussy, Byron in her mouth and Boy in her ass. The girl, Sunny Daze, was Tammi.

"The one you are watching is the mildest of the six. One of them has me doing a gangbang with nine men. One has me with a half a dozen blacks and the others are a mix of me with men and women doing all kinds of shit. In one of them I'm sitting in a bath tub with six men peeing on me while I laugh and rub it all over my skin.

"I'm not proud of what I did. I was drugged up or drunk most of the time, but you will notice that I seemed to be enjoying the hell out of it. That is because I was. The sex crazy woman on that screen is the same sex crazy woman who tries to fuck your eyes out of your head every night we go to bed. That was the problem. The girl on the screen and the girl here in the bedroom are one and the same.

"Jules found the tape when he visited an adult book store when he was in LA on business. After he found the first one he tracked down every video he could find that had Sunny Daze in it. The night I came home and found him watching the tape I thought my marriage was over, but it wasn't that way, at least not at first. Jules thought it was a hoot to have his very own porn star, but the more he watched the videos the more it had an effect on him. He watched me take on two, three or more at a time and saw me begging for more and he began thinking that one man wasn't enough for me. He got it fixed in his head that he couldn't satisfy me by himself and that since I wasn't climbing the walls in frustration or dragging him to the floor whenever I was with him that I must be getting the extra I needed somewhere else.

"He started accusing me of cheating on him behind his back. If I was a few minutes late in coming home it was because I was getting it on with a lover. If he called me at work and they told him I was in a meeting he just knew that they were covering for me while I was out getting a 'nooner.' If I was at home and he called and I didn't pick up right away it was because I had to pull myself away from my lover to get to the phone.

He started drinking and when he accused me of things I told him he was crazy and he called me a liar and hit me. One night he hit me several times and I called the police and they locked him up. He begged and pleaded with me to forgive him and he promised that he would never do it again so I didn't press charges and they let him go. Three weeks later he did it again and then another week later again and I called the police again and that time I pressed charges. The judge was reluctant to give Jules jail time so he gave him a suspended sentence on the condition he go into counseling. It seemed to work and things were good for the next five months and then I had to go out of town to a three day seminar in Denver. Jules called my room a couple of times and I wasn't there so he assumed I was in someone else's room and bed and when I came home he accused me of whoring around and when I denied it, he called me a lying slut and then hit me. From there it went on until what happened when he broke into the house."

"Okay, but what has all of that to do with me? Why did you show me that? That is in your past. It was before you met me and it is none of my business any more than what I did before you is yours."

"I had to show it to you. Jules found it by accident and you could have too. I don't want to get married again and go through what I went through with Jules."

"I would never do what he did to you."

"Maybe not the physical abuse part, but what about the disgust part? I know that I'm highly sexed and I know that there are nights when I exhaust you and still want more. You know it too. What will you start thinking when I have to work late and get sent out of town to seminars and conferences? And what about parties and social events? I'm a good looking woman and I attract male attention. How long before you start thinking that maybe I'm slipping off to meet one, two or three of them? How long before you start thinking that since I'm always wanting more I'm out trying to get it?"

"It would never happen because I know you Tammi and you aren't that kind of woman. I know that if I put my trust in you that it won't be misplaced."

"You say that now Henry, but don't forget that Jules was absolutely perfect for me at one time and he changed. You are perfect now, but what you now know can and probably will change you too. If you do and we aren't married we can just walk away."

I just looked at her and shrugged. "Thank you for being up front with me about this, but it doesn't change anything. If anything it just adds one more reason to the list of things that make it necessary to find me my own place."

"One more reason?"

"Yes Tammi, besides the ones I've already mentioned we can now add lack of trust to the list. You don't want to marry me because you don't trust me and I can't live with someone who doesn't trust me."

"Damn it Henry, I don't want you to move."

"Maybe not Tammi, but I think that it will be for the best."

***

I found a three bedroom condo that I liked, bought it and moved in. I turned one of the bedrooms into a den and home office and settled in. I kept in touch with Tammi and we dated a couple of times a week and the dates usually ended in her bedroom or mine. I guess Tammi found another guy because she started turning me down when I called and asked her out so after a couple of weeks I stopped calling. The condo complex had a pool and an exercise room and I started spending time at both. The complex also had quite a few single women living in it and I met several of them when I used the pool and exercise room. I dated eight or nine, bedded three, but there was no spark between any of us so for the most part we were just friendly neighbors.

One morning I met Carol in the exercise room, asked her out and we dated a couple of times before falling in bed together. Again there was no spark that would lead to a long term relationship, but we did like each other so we ended up seeing each other two or three times a week.

It might have gone on like that for years except one night I came home from spending three hours in Carol's bed to find Tammi sitting on my front steps. I invited her in and after seating her on the couch I asked if she would like a drink and she said white wine if I had it. I got her a glass and then I asked her how she'd been.

"Miserable. Things haven't been right for me since you moved out. When you left you left a big hole."

"It couldn't have been too bad. You did stop seeing me you know."

"Yes and it was a stupid move on my part. As much as I wanted you I still needed a full-time man and dating you a couple of times a week wasn't getting it for me. Since you wouldn't be my full-time guy anymore I decided that I needed to date others to see if maybe I could find one who could take your place. I didn't feel that I could do that if I stayed tied to you even partially. I dated a dozen or so guys since then Henry and I've come to realize that you just couldn't be replaced. I'm here tonight to beg you to take me back."

"A dozen or so guys?"

"Yes Henry, a lot of men and you know my sexual nature so I know what you are thinking and you are right."

She opened her purse, took out a paper and handed it to me. "I had that done when I finally accepted that I was going to have to crawl over here and beg."

I looked at the paper and saw that it was a form stating that Tammi had been tested and had been found to be free of any social diseases. I handed it back to her and said:

"This is kind of awkward."

"What?"

"I guess I'll have to get one of these for you."

"Does that mean you will have me back?"

"I don't know Tammi. If by having you back you mean go back to what we had I don't think so."

"Put any conditions on it you want Henry and I'll accept them. I just want you back."

***

Tonight I'm picking Tammi up from one of her charity meetings and we are going out for dinner, some drinks and dancing to celebrate our fifth wedding anniversary. As I was driving over to pick her up I thought about the last five years and some of the things that Tamm had worried about. She is still the sexual dynamo that she has always been and she does exhaust me and I know that there have been times – more than just a few I'm afraid – that I have left her wanting just a bit more. I've not become a Jules. I don't doubt her when she says she has to work late and I know that she is behaving herself when she goes out of town.

I'll never say it out loud or even let her suspect that I've even had the thought, but there are times when she leaves me lying on the bed a physical wreck that I almost wish she would stray a time or two and take the pressure off of me.

~~The End~~

Here is a sample from another story you may enjoy!

JUST PLAIN BOB

BUYING MY WIFE

Adult Erotica

The first thing I did when I got back to my office was get out the Yellow Pages and turn to Investigators and Investigative Services. There were three within two blocks of my office and the first two I called couldn't see me for three or four days but the third one said, "Come on down." As I walked the two blocks to Acme Investigative Services I tried to think of what Hargrove must have been smoking. There was no way that Abby could be having an affair with him let alone be planning on marrying him. We were too happy together. We had a great relationship, but at the same time I couldn't help but feel that something made Hargrove approach me and the best way to find out what it was was to put someone on the case to check things out. Maybe Abby was just a good friend and he misunderstood her feelings. For my own peace of mind I needed to find out what was going on.

I met with Mr. Owen Paulson and filled him in on my meeting with Hargrove. I told him that I seriously doubted that my wife was being unfaithful, but I did need to know what Hargrove was up to. The only times Abby was out of the house were for her Tuesday night book club and discussion group, her Thursday night bridge club meeting and her Saturday morning beauty shop appointment to have her hair done while I played golf with three of my friends. I gave Paulson all the information he asked for regarding Abby and then I gave him a check to get him started. Since it was a Wednesday he told me they would put an operative on Abby Thursday morning when she left the house to go to work and then watch her until the following Tuesday. He told me I could stop by or call him Wednesday for a report.

As I walked back to my office I spent more time trying to figure out what Hargrove was really after. I had absolutely no doubt about Abby's love for me, but I could not figure out for the life of me what Hargrove's angle was.

Abby usually beat me home and when I got home that night she was in the kitchen fixing dinner. She stopped what she was doing, came to me and put her arms around me and kissed me. Dinner and dishes out of the way we curled up on the couch to watch some TV and Abby moved in next to me, put her head on my shoulder and cuddled up next to me. This woman cheating on me? No way!

If you enjoyed this sample then look for **<u>Buying My Wife</u>**.

Also by this Author:

The Prodigal Family: The Abbotts

Watching My Shared Wife

The Waitress and the Runaway Husband

Baiting Mr. Little

Too Hot for Henry

Chuck's Fantasy

The Redhead's Desires

Rescued at Riley's

His Every Fantasy

Open Mike Night

Pursuit for Revenge

Why Does He Do That?

Halloween & Drugs

Tracey

When Rob Met Kari

Becoming a Shared Wife, Vol. 1 –
(Wife Sharing and Other Adventures)

Becoming a Shared Wife, Vol. 2 –
(Hazardous Wives)

Becoming a Shared Wife, Vol. 3 –
(Wives Who Stray)

Becoming a Shared Wife, Vol. 4 –

(Fulfilling Her Needs)

Becoming a Shared Wife, Vol. 5 –

(Rachel)

Becoming a Shared Wife, Vol. 6 –

(Sharing My Wife)

Becoming a Shared Wife, Vol. 7 –

(Sarah)

Becoming a Shared Wife, Vol. 8 –

(Cuckolds & Shared Wives)

Becoming a Shared Wife, Vol. 9 –

(Her Forbidden Fantasy)

A Just Plain Bob Christmas

Barbara Jean

Filthy Steps in the Office

My Perfect Wife: And Her Dirty Little Steps

Annabelle Gets Caught

All Filled Up!

Patio with a View

Boyfriend's Corrupted Steps

Never Never

His Wife's Doppelganger

Just A Back-up Guy

Secret Revenge

Erotica Short Stories, Vol. 8 –

(Wild Urges)

Erotica Short Stories, Vol. 9 –

(Horny)

Erotica Short Stories, Vol. 10 –

(Stuffed Hard)

Erotica Short Stories, Vol. 11 –

(9 Shades of Sex)

Erotica Short Stories, Vol. 12 –

(Doing What She Does Best)

Erotica Short Stories, Vol. 13 –

(Hottest Nights)

A Weird One

Blackmailed MILF

Filthy Steps With My...

The Biggest She's Ever Had

Sharing Penny

Hardest Nights

My Woman's Dirty Secrets

She Makes Me...

She Needs More

My Wife's Inferno

Dirty Love

Hot & Tight

Her Illicit Adventures

What I Want To Do To Her

Too Fun To Give Up

Creamed

Stepping Out

Hottest Wife

Naughty Wives

Deepest and Darkest

More Than She Can Take

Jennifer's Toes

The More The Sexier

Spice Up

Cyndi

Naughty And Nice

House Of Lovers

Hungry For More

Sweet Revenge

Turning Mommies Wild: The Carriage Tales

Bought And Used

Get Me Off

The Gambler

Gail's Price

Family Affair

Buying My Wife

You may also like the books by these authors:

G. Stuart Crane

THE FLOG ZONE

PARANORMAL PRECOGNITION

BDSM Erotic Romance

John Peters didn't know what his first birth was like, but his second one was agonizing. He remembered the pain, the drowsy driver crossing lanes, the sounds of crushing and crumpling metal and glass, the fire, and the screaming of his lungs out as they were seared by the very air he breathed. This passed and he felt a new sensation of someone using his/her hands to move his legs. Then came the hot kiss of a lash, and he felt as if he were being flogged forever when he tried to open his eyes to scream. Then the pain turned to pleasure and as it continued till the lash fell.

The scream came out as a gurgle, a whisper. His eyes opened to see light blue walls all around him and that he was in a bed. A woman in surgical scrubs was moving his legs and feet, stretching them, moving them back and forth at the ankles and knees. The woman was pleasant, not pretty in the formless clothes she wore, but with her red hair back in a short ponytail. Expressive green eyes is now wide and watching him. She had stopped what she was doing and was watching a machine beside him. The steady *beep beep* was replaced by something wilder and erratic.

As soon as the woman lets go of his foot, the sensation of being flogged stopped. The combined sensation of pain and pleasure stopped and the machine keeps beeping at a faster pace. She had rushed to his side, and was watching him struggle to form words with his mouth that no longer seemed to work. The noises coming from his mouth were just gargles and hisses.

She left in a hurry and somehow the presence of the fast beeping machine beside him was not an acceptable trade. Still trying to form words, he croaked for help. Where the heck was he and what was happening?

He managed to move his head a little, and look towards left and right. He was in a hospital ward of some kind and bodies on beds were to the left and right of him. Still with IV bags on stands and tubes everywhere, he was sure that he was unmoved. He tried to move his arms and found his arms free and couldn't move a little, since he was so weak.

Minutes passed, the silence was incredible except for the steady drone of the machines and the low beeping noises from all around him. The silence was replaced by the sound of footfalls. He heard hard soled shoes and squeaky rubber ones on tiled floors, walking in a hurry. A nurse in a white uniform and a man in a lab coat flapping behind were at his side. He was older, judging by the wrinkles and gray hair.

"You are awake?" the man in a lab coat asked.

He tried to say "Yes I am and where am I?" but all that came out was a series of croaks and guttural sounds. He did see a name embroidered on the lab coat stating that his name was D. Burns M.D.

He looked at John a few moments, then told the nurse to get some water and straw. He waited till she returned. He poured some room temperature water in a glass, added the straw, and held it to John's lips.

John sucked in the fluid and his mouth seemed to absorb it before the liquid got to his cheeks. The second pull on the straw was better and it got into his throat with the same effect. The third pull went down his throat and soon the dryness and tickling was gone. He pushed the straw away with his tongue and tried to speak again. This time, it came out in a whisper, but intelligible for his ears, it sounded weak and pitiful. "Where am I and how long have I been here?"

The Doctor had to lean closer to hear him. "We will get to that soon, but do you remember your name?"

John whispered his full name to the doctor, then sighed, this was going to be a memory test. Then, while he could, he rattled off his address and anything else that came to mind including his high school and college. The doctor pulled back to look at him. "And what's the last thing you remember?"

"Car, a big white SUV crossing the center line, I couldn't avoid it. I tried running my car onto the sidewalk, it happened fast, the fire, and me screaming." John managed to whisper. "What about my car?"

If you enjoyed this sample then look for The Flog Zone by G. Stuart Crane.

All Night Arcade

Jack Ryder

I have always enjoyed working at the arcade. Sort of a playground for adults so to speak. My wife Dana has never been real thrilled with my choice of employment. Especially since I work the night shift and don't get home till well after sunrise most mornings. Sometimes, not till after the lunch time hour.

I chose the night shift because you get much more "action" after dark! Usually a good mixed crowd of curious experimenters thrown together with a group of "here to play all night" folks. I usually do my best to see to it that the curiosity seekers have a good experience so they will want to return again...and again.

Sunday is the only day I have off. I would work that too if I were single, but the wife would cut my nuts off if I did not at least stay home ONE night each week. I have always found that each night has its own type of crowd. Monday is the lonely wife crowd. Tuesday and Thursday are the nights that are the slowest. But I fill that idle time by allowing the street girls to hang out and do what they do.

Friday and Saturday are the busiest nights and they keep me entertained best of all. Although the street girls do have a way of keeping me occupied on Tuesdays and Thursdays. But Wednesday night is what I have always called the mystery night. I am always busy but I just never know what is going to happen next or what kind of group will show up. It is sort of a "pot luck" crowd. And THAT can be very interesting!

Tonight was a typical Tuesday evening. I got most of my evening duties completed between
7 and 9pm as I normally do. During this time frame there is usually a slow shuffle of men that go back to the private booths to suck some cock through the glory holes. These are the wanna-be sort of men that are thrilled with the anonymity of having sex with other men without risking being seen by anyone else. Or having to admit to themselves that this thrills them so much.

It was just after nine when I saw her come into the front foyer leading into the main room. There are three separate areas in the arcade. The main room is the center part. It is where my customer counter is located. It is where the rows and rows of DVD racks are, the rows and rows of sexy apparel and the glass display counters with all the adult sex toys. There are four hidden cameras that cover the main area. The video screen is behind the counter where I can keep an eye on everything. I was watching her from all four angles as she slowly made her way towards me at the counter. She was gorgeous!

"My name's Dixie, Hun!" She was bent over the counter before I could stick out a hand to greet her properly. Her fluffy collared jacket fell open enough to expose her bare breasts to me. My eyes were riveted to her tits as she continued to look down into the glass like she was looking at the dildos in the case. "I'm new here and the other girls said you are nice to us working gals." Her eyes moved upward to catch me staring at her lovely 36CC globes.

Dixie placed her elbows on the glass but did not adjust her jacket or try to stand up. Her tits were nearly right in my face. "You gunna be nice to me, darlin?" She had a gleam in her eye as she said it and a subtle little grin. "I could be...so nice to you!" She reached over and laid her hand on my arm. "Do you get a break around this joint?" she whispered as she stood up but leather coat wide open. "Somewhere private...where we could...enjoy ourselves?"

Dixie pulled her jacket closed as we heard the doorbell dingle to announce the arrival of two younger men. They took a quick look at her but then hurried to the booths on the eastside of the building. Dixie was smiling sweetly as I dialed my cell phone. "George...can you...cover for me about an hour!" She was now petting my arm softly as I glanced down at her gorgeous shapely legs. The indecently short mini skirt barely covered her honey pot and her thighs looked yummy.

I sat down on the couch across from my desk as she opened her jacket and let it fall to the floor. "So, Dixie...what did you have in mind?" I teased her as I kicked off my shoes.

"I intend to rock your world!" she said it softly as she unzipped her skirt and let it fall to her ankles. Dixie was now standing in front of me in only her garter belt, black sheer stockings and stiletto heels. "That way you will always be willing to have me back!" She stepped right in front of me and I was looking straight up into her dripping wet gash.

"Oh, Dixie, look at that!" I whispered as I reached up to run a finger up her slit.

If you enjoyed this sample then look for **All Night Arcade** by **Jack Ryder.**

HOT ROMANCE

A GIRL CALLED

Len

KERRY JAMES

I fumbled my way through the dark club, apologising to the patrons as I stepped on toes, or bumped them and eventually found a seat quite close to the stage. I had paid a lot of money to be here, and I was going to get my money's worth. The stripper sort of danced to the recorded music, and gradually divested herself of her clothes. These she threw backwards to the wings of the stage. When she was down to just her skimpy panties, she stopped stripping and just sort of danced around the stage. At last, she started to slip them down, turning her back on the audience as they dropped below her hips. At that point, she wiggled and they fell to her ankles. Stepping out of them, she kicked them back to the wings, and then turned to face the audience, keeping one hand over the juncture of her thighs, listening to the music. At last, as the music came to its finale, she stood perfectly still with her legs tightly together and took her hand away, allowing us to see her pubic hair, but nothing else. She remained like that for about five seconds then the spotlights went out and the curtain drew.

I was to learn later that there were stringent rules as to what the girl could do and show on stage, and what she could not. I watched about three acts and whilst the way they got there varied, the last few seconds of the show were always the same. I knew that there were ten girls performing that night, and I was going to watch all of them. I was actually getting bored after seeing five or six of them, but I had paid to see the ten, I was bloody well going to see them. As patrons had left and seats became available I had managed to get nearer the stage, and just before the next act, a bloke got up from the very front and left. I was first into his still warm vacant seat.

Then the disembodied voice announced the next girl. "Ladies and gentlemen, we are proud to present the lovely Lee!" It seemed stupid to me to announce ladies and gentlemen, there was little chance of any women being in the audience. The curtains drew back and the spots came on to highlight the next stripper. Suddenly I went cold. My mind was playing tricks. It did look like her, but it couldn't be, I must be mistaken; after all, it was ten years since we last saw each other. She would have changed, and she would never be here taking her clothes off for a load of dirty old men. The irony that I was one among the forty or so of the dirty old men, passed me by completely. My front row seat meant that at certain times, as the moveable spot followed the girl around, my face would come into the splash of light. It was just what happened as the girl looked in my direction, and her face was shaken out of the bland uninterested look that all the girls seem to wear. Her routine took her away, but she looked over her shoulder as if to be certain. Then she turned in her dance, which had to be said was superior to the other dancers, and looked again.

At last, she seemed to come to a decision, so the next time she came to my side of the stage, she maneuvered much closer than before. She looked down at me, and from the side of her mouth a question came, "Danny?"

If you enjoyed this sample then look for <u>A Girl Called Len</u> by Kerry James.

The Square Circle
MURDER IS THE NAME OF THE GAME
SEDUCTIVE SUSPENSE
Amy Redek

The cafeteria, as expected, was crowded. The queue wasn't as long as Francis thought as she picked up her tray and joined the end of it. Francis Mann didn't mind the bustle of the city, coming from the small town of Malden in Essex. She had driven into Chelmsford with her husband, and they had travelled down by train that morning to London. Him to go to work while she went on this shopping expedition. Francis was just past her thirty-ninth birthday, dreading the next one, but was happy that she could still pass for a late twenty-year-old. Her figure, while not exactly hourglass, was still trim in spite of giving birth to a daughter twenty years previously. Her bust was nice and matronly and her legs were still slender that finished down at size five shoes. Ash blonde hair that didn't seem to need brushing at any time, framed a face once described as beautiful but now called very pretty. The pencilled eyebrows above soft brown eyes that had only a hint of mascara so as not to be distractive, led down to a short, but straight nose above her soft lips.

Behind her in the queue stood Penelope Swithers, though she always preferred to be known as Penny. She was only out that day because she was bored at home. Home being a house in Knightsbridge, so she hadn't travelled very far to be in the store. Penny was thirty years old and looked like a model in her trim suit having the figure that you would never see on a catwalk. Top heavy was her own description of herself, but from there down, perfect. She too was blonde, but tending more to the brunette colour than that of Francis before her in the queue. Her face was long but balanced by the wide blue eyes and generous mouth separated by her nose that on a round-faced person would have been large, but suited her perfectly.

Francis reached the till and paid for her tea, pastry and small chocolate bar, and moved off. Penny paid for her coffee, a slice of cake and a peach, and followed on through the crowded tables and nearly lost the lot when Francis suddenly stopped to turn round.

'Oh sorry,' said Francis, seeing the tray Penny was carrying, nearly tilt the contents off. 'I didn't realise anyone was behind me. This place is so full I can't see an empty seat.'

'There's an empty table over there,' Penny said, indicating with her chin across the shoulder of Francis.

'Oh you're right,' she replied after looking round, 'let's grab it quick before anyone else.'

They moved quickly between the other full tables, neatly swerving around crooked elbows and side stepping the bags and parcels that were in every little aisle. The table was in a corner and had just been vacated, but was still littered with trays and used crockery and other debris.

'Here, hold my tray a moment,' Penny said, handing her tray to Francis as they reached the table. 'I'll clear this off for us.'

Francis stood with both trays in her hands while Penny scooped all the litter onto two of the trays and looking round, but not finding anywhere they could go, gave a grin to Francis and pushed them between the two long flower troughs that bordered the eating area.

'Let them pick those up later,' she smiled, taking her tray back and sitting down. Francis pulled out a chair and setting her tray on the table, sat down opposite.

Two other women saw the table being cleared and both made a beeline for the two vacant seats that were there. The first was Anne Seymour, and apart from her hair being a soft brown, could have been the bookend for Penny, her figure being almost the same. She was big breasted above a trim waist and had long slim legs with well-rounded calves, and like Penny, was only thirty years old.

'May I join you?' she asked of Francis and Penny, standing by the table.

'By all means,' Francis replied with a slight wave of the hand, and Anne put her tray down and sat next to her.

'Can I too?' asked Jane, eyeing the last seat and having heard Anne ask the question.

'Certainly,' said Penny, removing her handbag from the last chair. With a sigh, Jane gratefully sank down on the seat beside her.

'Hi! I'm so glad to get off my feet. My name's Jane. Short for Jane,' she said with a little laugh. 'Yours?' was the query left in the air.

'Anne.'

'Francis.'

'Penny.'

'Well it's nice to meet you. I've just had a bellyful of this place. Worse than Epsom on Derby day. Bet you've never seen a crowd like this before in here?' Jane was married to a book-maker, hence her manner of speech and outgoing personality. London born and bred, she oozed the very spirit of a person raised within the sounds of Bow Bells. Short sharp pithy words and quick head movements like a pigeon constantly looking out for signs of danger. Shorter than the others, but not by much.

Again, thirty years old, but with her round face framed by her black hair at shoulder length, looked younger, except for the little lines at the corner of the eyes that only another woman would see to guess her age correctly. Her figure was slimmer than the others' and not quite in proportion having smaller breasts, thicker waist and fuller hips. Too much eating in restaurants or from hot dog stands at racetracks was not a healthy way to eat.

'It is a trifle crowded,' Anne admitted, sipping her tea, 'I only came to get out of the house for a while.'

'Me too. All day cooped up, never seeing anyone gets you really depressed,' replied Penny.

'I can spend all day in the garden and still not see a soul go past,' chipped in Francis.

'Where do you live then?' asked Penny.

'Just outside the village of Malden, in Essex,' she replied.

'An Essex girl!' sniggered Jane.

'Not at all,' Francis replied indignantly, 'I was born in Sussex. My husband was born in Essex though.'

'Do the old jokes apply to them too?' enquired Penny with a straight face, but a hint of a smile at her lips.

'I think so,' was the laughing reply, 'boring, and as much sex appeal as a lamppost,' nibbling on her pastry.

'That's the trouble with my husband. Too much sex appeal. I never see the bastard much these days,' said Penny gloomily, looking down into her empty cup. 'I wish one of his popsie's would take him off my hands. The divorce settlement would suit me down to the ground.'

'Well I see mine too much. I'm dragged from racecourse to racecourse. But then, when I don't go, I hear he has some tart with him. Yes, a divorce settlement would sort me out too!' Jane put in.

'Humph,' snorted Anne, 'if my husband saw another woman, he wouldn't know what to do. He wouldn't have the time anyway. You can set your watch by his habits. Divorce would be no good to me, he's worth more with his life insurance.'

Pushing her empty plate a little and dabbing at her lips with a tissue, Francis said, 'I'm in the same boat there, though I'm worth more dead to him than he is to me. Must sort that out one day, then maybe it would be worthwhile having him bumped off!' She gave a little hiccup. 'Oh do excuse me,' she said with a little laugh.

'I wish someone would do that for me,' Penny said wistfully.

'Kill him you mean?' asked Jane.

'Why not? He might just as well be dead for what I see of him. Besides, I wouldn't waste money like he does.'

'I don't get any money, well not much to speak of. For this shopping trip I have to use a credit card with a limit given me by my husband!' said Anne.

'That *is* the limit,' declared Jane, and then in a musing tone, 'I could take over the bookmaking and keep all the money myself. Or take in a partner. Perhaps you, Penny. Instead of his slogan, "A pound for a Pound," we could make it "In for a Penny, in for a Pound."' She laughed gaily, and the others did too.

'What about you, Anne?' asked Penny, 'No credit card limit. The sky would be the limit.'

'I don't know,' she said, absently stirring her spoon round in an empty cup before realising what she was doing, letting the spoon drop clattering into the saucer. 'It would be foolish to try. You'd be the first suspect after taking out a hefty insurance and then he's popped off. Well, you know what I mean.'

'Not if you were somewhere else and had a cast iron alibi,' Jane said. 'I mean if it looked like he died as a result of an accident.'

'I wouldn't mind if somebody else did it,' Anne popped in.

Jane gave a little flutter of her hands, indicating for the others to lean forward closer. The heads of all four moved closer to the centre of the table as she whispered, 'What if we got together and did it ourselves? Knock them off at different times, different places, and all that?'

Then they all leaned back and gave serious looks to each other, the silence around the table very deafening within the café's hubbub. Jane leaned forward again.

'Let's not say anymore on this now. What I suggest is that if we are interested, let's meet again in about a month's time, say at the wine bar next door for lunch, and then talk? Say about one o'clock?'

She looked at Penny who nodded straight away. Francis, after a slight hesitation, then at Anne, who flushed with the three pairs of eyes on her, and dropping her own eyes, slowly nodded, and so an agreed date and time was set.

'Well,' Penny said. 'As I live here in London, shall I book a table for then?'

'Good idea,' Jane replied.

'My God, is that the time!' Anne exclaimed. 'I've got to get home. He has to have his dinner on the table at exactly six fifteen.' As she grabbed at her handbag and carrier bag, Jane caught hold of her wrist.

'Think what it would be like if you didn't have to rush, ever again,' she whispered softly, slowly letting go. 'See you next month?'

'Maybe you will,' she replied, 'maybe I will see you all. Bye for now.' Then with a flurry of coat and bag, she left the table and made her way out of the café.

'I'd better make a move too,' said Jane, 'maybe I'll catch the bastard in bed with one of his tarts and do the job myself.'

'Without the insurance?' Penny asked.

'You're right! See you next month then, and, oh,' she gave a throaty chuckle, 'I forgot. There's a horse in the three forty five tomorrow.

Put your shirt on it. It's hot at twenty to one.' She picked up her things and was just leaving the table.

'What's the name?' queried Francis.

"Blood Money," Jane laughed as she left.

'Well if that horse comes in I'll see it as an omen and be here next month,' Francis said, putting out her hand. Penny took it and said softly,

'See you next month.'

Ironically, the horse did win…

If you enjoyed this sample then look for **The Square Circle by Amy Redek.**

Hot Erotica
George X. Bush

DESIRED
by the Boys

IN THE CABIN

Mary was fed up with being left behind each month while Riley went up to the cabin with his three friends, Mark, Robert, and John, to fish, drink and just have fun. She was only 23 and she wanted some fun, too. She resented being left behind to fend for herself in this way. She poured herself another drink, her third, and flopped down onto the sofa in frustration as she sipped her drink. *I'll show him*, she thought, sipping her drink, a plan coming into her head. Quickly gulping the rest of her drink down, Mary went to her room and quickly threw a change of clothes and some toiletries into a bag, grabbing her pocketbook and keys as she locked the door behind her and got into the car. If she drove steadily, she could be there in three hours and surprise them.

Mary had to stop a couple of times on the way as she felt herself getting tired, but she finally pulled up to the cabin around four in the morning. As she let herself in, she heard the sounds of snoring coming from different areas of the cabin. She was tired and felt a bit ragged from all she had drunk during the evening, so she quietly tiptoed to the bathroom to take a shower. The water felt so good after the long drive and she stood under it enjoying the sensation.

When she got out of the shower and dried herself, she appraised what she was seeing in the mirror. Her long red hair hung down to the middle of her back. She had that pale skin with light freckles that was common to redheads. Her breasts were very full with large pale nipples on the ends. Mary cupped them in her hands, gently squeezing them as her fingers automatically sought out and found her nipples, squeezing them and pinching them, pulling on them as they screwed themselves into large hard knots. Her hands trailed down her flat stomach to where a small thatch of bright red pubic hair used to grow above her pussy. She had no hair on her pussy, having had it removed by electrolysis so that it was as smooth as a baby's. At the top of her slit, her clit hood peeked through her pussy lips and her clit, fat as a pinkie finger, stuck out from beneath its hood. Her hand trailed down and her fingers trailed up through and between her pussy lips, feeling herself and the wetness that was starting. Her legs were long and straight, as were her feet and toes. Men had always found her beautiful and at the moment she quite agreed with them.

She was still squeezing her breasts with one hand, her other still between her legs when suddenly the door opened and Robert staggered in, completely naked, his cock dangling in front of him, bigger than anything Mary had ever imagined. As he shut the door, he blinked his eyes, trying to clear the fog of alcohol and sleep so he could make sense of what he was seeing.

"Mary?" he croaked, his voice still sounding a bit drunk.

"Hi, Robert," Mary said, frozen where she stood, her hands not moving.

"What're you doin' here?" he asked, slurring his words. "And how come you're naked?"

"Uh, I thought I'd drive up and surprise Riley and I just took a shower," she replied, letting her hands fall to her sides as she stared at his cock which was beginning to grow even larger…

If you enjoyed this sample then look for **Desire By The Boys** by George X. Bush.

WANT FREE COPIES OF MY BOOKS?

Just visit my blog and download free copies of my books:

awesomeauthors.org/justplainbob